Bella
Gets Her Skates On

For Sophia and Amélie, with love – I.W.

To Peter and Mia, with love – R.R.

First published 2007 by Macmillan Children's Books
This edition published 2011 by Macmillan Children's Books
a division of Macmillan Publishers Limited
20 New Wharf Road, London N1 9RR
Basingstoke and Oxford
Associated companies throughout the world
www.panmacmillan.com

ISBN: 978-1-4472-0269-1

Text copyright © Ian Whybrow 2007
Illustrations copyright © Rosie Reeve 2007
Moral rights asserted.

1 3 5 7 9 8 6 4 2

A CIP catalogue record for this book
is available from the British Library.

Printed in China

Ian Whybrow

Bella
Gets Her Skates On

Illustrated by Rosie Reeve

MACMILLAN CHILDREN'S BOOKS

Daddy Rabbit liked making up funny names for his little rabbits. Ben was always in a hurry, so Daddy called him Big Brother Rushabout.

Sophie was super neat, so Daddy called her Big Sister Tidypaws.

As for little Bella, she worried a lot.
So Daddy called her Little Baby Not-Sure.

One winter's morning Daddy said,
"Who wants to go ice skating today?
The lake is frozen hard!"

"Me me me!"
said Ben.

"Me me me!"
said Sophie.

But Bella was worried about skating.
What if she looked silly and everyone laughed at her?
"I'm not sure," she said.

"Don't worry, Little Baby Not-Sure," said Daddy.
"Eat a good breakfast and then you'll be ready
for skating."

"I'm having *two* smoothies
for breakfast," said Ben.
"I'm a speedy eater!"
"Well done, Big Brother
Rushabout!" said Daddy.

Sophie ate up all her fruit and
yoghurt without spilling one bit.
"Well done, Big Sister Tidypaws!"
said Daddy.

But Bella just played with her porridge and she wouldn't eat her eggy soldiers. She still wasn't sure about skating. She only had little legs. What if she couldn't keep up?

Straight after breakfast Daddy said,
"Come on, little rabbits! Let's get ready
to go out."

"I'm the fastest!" said Ben.
"Well done, Big Brother
Rushabout!" said Daddy.

"And I look the smartest!" said Sophie.
"That's right, Big Sister Tidypaws!"
said Daddy.

But Bella wouldn't put her hat and scarf on.

She still wasn't sure about skating.
What if she fell over and hurt herself?

So Daddy said, "Don't worry, Little Baby Not-Sure.
Let's just have some fun in the snow first."
"Yes! Let's all make a snow-rabbit!" shouted
Ben and Sophie.

So Bella went outside with the others.
But instead of making a snow-rabbit . . .

. . . she made a snow-mouse!
That made everybody laugh.
"Well done, my Funny Bunny!"
said Daddy.

Then Ben and Sophie wanted to go sledging.
"Good idea!" said Daddy. "All aboard!"
And before Bella had time to start worrying,
off they went, sliding over the snow.

Soon they were rushing down the hill with the wind whooshing in their ears. But suddenly they came to a bumpy bit.

Up in the air went Ben and Sophie.

And down they went – plop – into a snowdrift!

But Bella held on tight
all the way to the bottom.
She didn't fall off at all!
"Well done, my Slippy Slider!"
laughed Daddy.

They stopped at the edge of the lake
and Daddy said, "Skates on, everyone!"
But Bella was worried again.

What a VERY BIG lake it was!
And what a lot of skaters!

So Bella just sat and watched with Daddy.
Then she said, "Look at that funny bunny! I was a
funny bunny when I made my snow-mouse, wasn't I?"
"Yes, you were!" laughed Daddy.

"And look at that slippy slider!
I was a slippy slider when I stayed
on the sledge, wasn't I?"
"You were the *best* Slippy Slider!"
laughed Daddy.

That made Bella feel a lot
more sure of herself.
"Maybe I can be a
skater too!" she said.

So she laced up her boots,

and one paw . . .

two paws . . .

she stepped on to the ice!

And she went SSSSslip!

She went SSSSslide!

And suddenly . . . Bella was skating!

"This is FUN!" she shouted.

"Well done, Bella!" called Daddy.

"You're a super skater!" said Ben and Sophie.

After the skating was over, Daddy said
they could all have hot chocolate.
So Ben ran and fetched some extra quick!
"Well done, Big Brother Rushabout!"
said Daddy.

Sophie did the pouring
and she didn't spill a drop.
"Well done, Big Sister Tidypaws!"
said Daddy.

Bella drank a great big mugful
and said it was the BEST EVER.
"Well done, my little
Super Skater!" said Daddy.

And as they walked home
Daddy said, "Wasn't skating fun today!
Who wants to go again tomorrow?"
"Me me me!" said Ben.
"Me me me!" said Sophie.

But Bella said, "I'm not sure . . ."
"Not sure about skating?" asked Daddy.

"No! I'm not sure I can wait till tomorrow!"
laughed Bella.

"Three cheers for Bella!"
said Ben and Sophie.

"Hip hip hooray!" said Daddy.

And do you know, he didn't call
her Little Baby Not-Sure
ever again!